MW01591560

Don't Eat Doctor Peanut!

Six Nutty Tales

by Alan Venable

ONE MONKEY BOOKS

San Francisco

One Monkey Books
156 Diamond Street
San Francisco, CA 94114
415-863-8150
OneMonkeyBooks.com

This is a work of fiction. Resemblance to actual persons is coincidental and unscientific.

Teachers and parents: find thoughtful suggestions at OneMonkeyBooks.com. For generous multi-copy discounts, contact:

Publisher@OneMonkeyBooks.com

ISBN 978-0-9777082-9-1

For Adriane Lonzarich

And for Ember, Misha and
Annika

Not forgetting Steve

With special thanks to Avalon,
Sasha and Dean

Chapters

Chapter 1

Meet the Doctor

Get ready to meet the smallest doctor in the world. Get set to meet Doctor Peanut. He is waiting for you to say hello. ->

But how do you greet a peanut who might not even speak English? Peanuts can talk, but they speak a language called *Pinglish*. So you can't just stick out your hand and say, "Nice to meet you." You need to say, "*Nutty* to meet you."

That is a greeting a peanut would understand. But what would Dr. Peanut do next? I'm not sure. Up to now, the talking peanuts are mostly afraid of giants like us. So he might dive into the nearest bush. But Dr. Peanut isn't just any talking peanut. He's a doctor after all! So what else might he do? He might just stick out his hand and say, "*Nutty* to meet you, too."

I know what you're thinking. You're thinking, "*Talking* peanuts? Peanuts can't talk!"

Well, I don't mean the peanuts you buy to eat. I don't mean the roasted, salted ones. Of course, a roasted peanut can't talk! *You couldn't talk either if someone roasted and salted your brain.* It takes *nutty* brains to be able to talk. It takes *nutty* brains also to be a doctor because doctors need to be able to think.

Dr. Peanut is the kind of doctor who looks after kids. In *Pinglish*, they call him a *peanutrician*. He keeps all the peanut kids *nutty*.

Suppose you were a peanut kid and went to him for a check-up. The first thing he might say is this:

"How are you? You look *nutty* today! May I listen to your kernels?"

If you said, "Okay," then the *peanutrician* would listen to your kernels. If they sounded strong, he might say, "*Nutty!*" If they sounded ill, he might say, "Oh my! Are you feeling *peavish*?"

If the *peavish* kid has a cold, the doctor holds out a hanky and says, "Here, try blowing your nose."

If you have a sore throat, the doctor might give you a spoonful of honey.

Dr. Peanut lives a *nutty* life, but he does have one big problem. He needs to be careful when he goes out. He needs to stay out of sight of the giants. Why? I bet you can guess.

What do giants do with peanuts?

Chomp!

So when talking peanuts go out, they try to fool the giants. They dress up to look like things that giants don't eat. Sometimes they dress up as mice. (Most giants don't eat mice.)

Sometimes they hide by carrying tree leaves on their heads. (Most giants don't eat the leaves off trees.)

One day, Dr. Peanut dresses up like an ant, because most giants

don't eat ants. Then he goes for a walk
in the park. But the doctor is going to
learn two big lessons. The first lesson is
that there are squirrels in the park, and
squirrels *love* to eat peanuts. The second
lesson is that *squirrels are harder to fool
than giants.*

In the park, a squirrel
sees the doctor. It
bounces toward
him across the
grass. Dr.
Peanut tries
to run, but
peanuts can't
run as fast as
squirrels. Then
he sees a candy

wrapper that some careless giant dropped.
He crawls inside the wrapper to hide.

He waits there, hiding, hoping the
squirrel will go away. He waits....

And waits.

And waits.

When he thinks the squirrel is gone, he looks out to see if he is safe.

Suddenly, a giant hand scoops him out of the wrapper and lifts him into the sky.

Two giant kids have found him. They stare at him with big, bright eyes. Their mouths are huge and terrible!

"Stop!" the doctor cries.

"Did someone say something?" asks one of the giants. She looks around.

"I did," yells the doctor.

"Who said that?" asks the other giant. He also looks around.

"Me! Me!" yells Dr. Peanut.

"Oh!" says one of the giants. "We could hardly hear you."

"Then open your ears!" the doctor yells.

"And shut your mouths and let me go. I really don't want you to eat me!"

"Eat you?" says the giant boy. "Why would we eat you? You were in that wrapper, but you aren't a piece of candy."

"Right," says the doctor. "As you can see, I'm an ant. You can tell by the feelers I'm wearing."

The giants don't seem to believe him. They don't look fooled.

"Are you kidding?" says the boy.

The girl licks her lips. "I think I'm getting hungry," she says.

"Me, too," says the boy.

They lick their lips. Dr. Peanut needs to think fast!

"Wait," he says. "You should never just pick things up in the park. And never eat things that you find on the ground. I'm a doctor, so I know."

"I found a strawberry on the ground, once," says the girl. "It was growing there, and I ate it."

"That's different," the doctor replies. "Strawberries are meant to be eaten, but *pease, pease*, never eat ants. Or peanuts. Never! *Pease!*"

"Never eat *peas*?" asks the girl.

Dr. Peanut wonders if he needs to check her ears. He is sure he did not tell her not to eat peas!

"Some people eat ants," says the boy. "I read that in a book. It said that ants taste spicy. But those people don't live around here."

"Right," says the doctor. "So don't eat me!"

"But you're not an ant," says the boy.

"Oh, no? Okay, what am I?"

Doc hopes they think he is some kind of bug.

"You're a peanut."

"No, I'm not."

"You are."

"Oh? How can you be sure?" asks the doctor. "I *might* be a peanut, but maybe not."

He thinks as fast as he can about how to get the giants to think of something other than food. Then he has a new idea.

He says, "Maybe I *am* a peanut, but I am also a doctor, so you both should do as I say. Let me check to see how *nutty* you are. Stick out your tongues and say, 'Aaaah.'"

The giants stick out their tongues.

"Aaaah," they say.

The doctor looks in their mouths. He taps their teeth to hear how they sound.

Then he tells them, "I'm glad to say,

you both sound *nutty*, but you might get sick if you eat me now, because you could spoil your supper."

"Is that really true?" asks the boy.

"Maybe not," says the doctor, "but you could also have an allergy to peanuts. If you are allergic to peanuts, one taste of me could make you very *peavish*."

"What does *peavish* mean?" asks the girl.

"Well, in this case it would mean you get sick."

"We're not allergic to peanuts," says the girl. "We know that because we eat peanut butter all the time."

That is not what the doctor wanted to hear.

"And at Halloween," says the boy, "we get roasted peanuts dipped in chocolate."

The kids rub their tummies.

Dr. Peanut feels more and more worried. He closes his eyes and sees himself being roasted. He sees himself being dipped in chocolate. He sees himself as peanut butter in a peanut-butter-and-jelly sandwich. What *peavish* thoughts! He must think of something to say to make these giants change their minds.

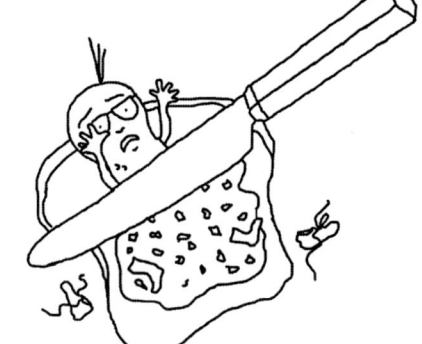

"I know what I will say," he thinks. "I'll ask these giants how they would feel if someone bit into *them!*"

He opens his eyes and says, "All right. Now tell me how you would feel if someone cracked *you* with their teeth."

"*Cracked* us?" asks the girl.

The boy laughs. "Oh! Did you think we were going to eat you?"

"Aren't you?" asks the doctor.

The boy makes a face. "Not me. I don't eat anything that talks."

"Me, neither," says the girl. "Do *you*?"

This makes the doctor feel much better. He says, "Me, neither, too! Ha ha!"

"We'll just put you back where we found you," she says.

"No, wait," says Dr. Peanut. "If you put me back in the grass, I think a squirrel might eat *me*. Could you take me home instead, *pease*?"

The girl laughs and says, "Did you say *pease* again? What kind of word is that?"

"It's *Pinglish*!"

"Really?" she replies. She thinks a moment and says, "Oh, now I know what you mean by that. Of course we'll take you home."

"*Nutty!*" the doctor replies.

On the way to the doctor's home, the giants

ask him lots of questions.

"Why did you dress up like an ant?" asks the girl. "Did you think tonight was Halloween?"

"No," he replies. "I don't even know what Halloween is, but talking peanuts dress up when they go out so they won't look like peanuts and giants won't eat us. You should see me dressed up like a lady bug. First, I paint myself red all over. Then I add some small black dots. And of course I wear my feelers."

The giants grin.

"You're *nutty*," says the girl.

Dr. Peanut grins. "You just spoke *Pinglish*. I can tell you learn fast."

"I have a *nutty* idea," says the boy. "Why don't you carry a megaphone? A megaphone would make you louder when you talk."

"What's a megaphone?" asks the doctor.

"I'll make you one," says the boy. "It's

small at one end and big at the other."

He picks up a scrap of paper, rolls it

like a funnel and gives it to the doctor.

"Talk into the small end," he tells Dr. Peanut.

The doctor holds the megaphone up to his mouth and says, "HELLO!"

His voice is so loud, the kids hold their ears.

"WHAT A SMART IDEA," says the doctor through his megaphone.

By now they are back at his house. He points down from a giant shoulder and says, "THAT'S WHERE I LIVE."

The giants set him down at his door. They get down on the ground to look inside.

"I WOULD INVITE YOU IN," says the doctor, "BUT I DON'T THINK YOU WOULD FIT."

"That's all right," they say. "Come over to our place sometime."

They shake hands and say, "*Nutty* to meet you."

Now Dr. Peanut has fewer problems out of doors. When he needs to step out, he often goes with his giant friends. Wherever he goes in the world of giants, he takes his megaphone, so he can warn them not to eat him. *Nutty!*

Chapter 2

Slimy

Dr. Peanut stays busy all week taking care of young peanuts.

(As you know, he is a *peanutrician*.) But on wet weekends, he sits at home alone. He lives by himself and he feels lonely.

One rainy Saturday, he puts

on his raincoat and boots to go visit his giant friends. He wears his megaphone as a hat.

When he arrives at the giants' house, the kids are glad to see him.

"Hi, Dr. Peanut," says the boy. "We weren't expecting you today. Come in and get dry."

"Thanks," the doctor replies. "I'm sorry, but I can't use my megaphone. It got soggy in the rain."

"That's okay," says the boy. "It's nice and quiet in here. We can hear you fine without it. Do you need some help today?"

"No," says the doctor. "I just didn't want to be by myself."

"Doctor, do you feel lonely a lot?" asks the girl.

"Not too much," he replies. "I only feel lonely when it rains all day and I get tired of reading and can't think of anything *nutty* to do."

"You should get a pet," says the boy.

"A pet?" says Dr. Peanut. "What's that?"

The giants laugh. The girl says, "We thought doctors knew everything! A pet is an animal friend."

"Oh, you mean a *peat*," Dr. Peanut replies. "That's what we call them in *Pinglish*."

"Really?" she says. "What kinds of animals do peanuts keep as *peats*?"

"Oh, lady bugs, fireflies and other critters," says the doctor.

"How about mice?" says the boy. He takes a mouse out of its cage. "They sure are cute."

"Don't mice eat peanuts?" the doctor asks.

"I forgot about that," says the boy. "I guess you don't really want to keep mice."

The girl pulls a kitten out from under the couch.

"How about a kitty?" she asks. "You could ride around on it like a horse. And I'm pretty sure they don't eat peanuts."

She picks up Dr. Peanut and puts him

on the kitten's back. But the kitten rolls over. Dr. Peanut falls off. Then the kitten bats him across the room.

"Help!" the doctor cries. "That tiger knocked off my glasses!"

The boy pulls the kitten away from the doctor. The girl helps him find his glasses.

Dr. Peanuts gets back on his feet and says, "A kitten may be a *nutty* pet, but it never would be the right kind of *peat*. To me, that kitten was *peavish!*"

The boy lifts the doctor up to a fish tank. "What about a fish for a *peat*?" he asks.

The giants put the doctor in a boat so he can float around in the tank. He stares down into the water.

"Do fish eat peanuts?" he asks.

"They might," says the boy.

"That's *peavish*," says the girl.

On the wall of the fish tank, down below the water line, the doctor sees a shell.

"What's that?" he asks.

"That? That's just a snail. It's there to eat the green stuff that grows on the glass."

"Green stuff?" says the doctor. Here is a chance for him to show the giant kids how much he really knows. It's his chance to make up for not knowing what they meant by pet.

He says, "That green stuff on the tank is a plant. In science, we call it algae."

The kids nod. "We already know that," they say.

By now, the rain has ended and it is time for the doctor to head on home. On his way, he has a *nutty* idea. He thinks, "I'll catch a baby snail for a *peat*!"

He stops at a *peat* shop and asks the clerk what a snail might eat if it lived on land.

"That's easy," says the clerk. "Just feed it corn meal and leafy foods like lettuce. Would you like to buy a snail?"

"I plan to catch my own," says the doctor. "Is there anything *peavish* about snails?"

"I don't think so," says the clerk. "May I show you a *nutty* thing about them?" He takes out a snail. "Look at the eyes on this one. See how the eyes of the snail are out at the ends of two long feelers? Now watch what happens if the snail thinks you might touch one of its eyes."

"Oh, dear," says the doctor. "I wouldn't want someone to touch *my* eye."

"Me, neither," says the clerk. "So just pretend like you want to touch it."

Dr. Peanut reaches toward one of the

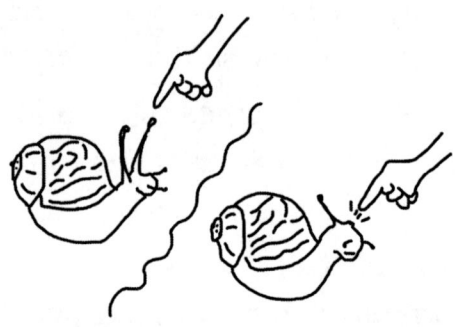

eyes. Quickly, the eye slides down into the
feeler. At the same time, the feeler slides
down inside the head of the snail.

"*Nutty!*" says the doctor.

That evening, Dr. Peanut finds a snail
in the yard and takes it inside for a *peat*.
He feeds it a nice leaf of lettuce.

"I'm going to call you Curly," he says.
"Can you guess why?"

The snail doesn't answer.

"How do you like that for a name?" asks
the doctor.

Curly chews on his lettuce. He smiles,
but he does not reply.

A few weeks pass. Each night, the

doctor measures Curly from the tip of his tail to the ends of his eyeballs. He learns that Curly is growing fast.

One night, Dr. Peanut tells Curly, "I think we are very much alike. For example, we are both a bit round, and we both have shells. I can hardly wait until you can talk."

Curly smiles but does not reply.

Then Dr. Peanut starts to have problems. For one thing, at bedtime, Curly never wants to sleep. In fact, he goes to sleep in the morning when the doctor is getting ready to work. When the doctor finishes work in the evening, Curly wants to play all night! Poor Dr. Peanut can't get a wink of sleep because Curly makes too much noise.

This snail is *peavish*!

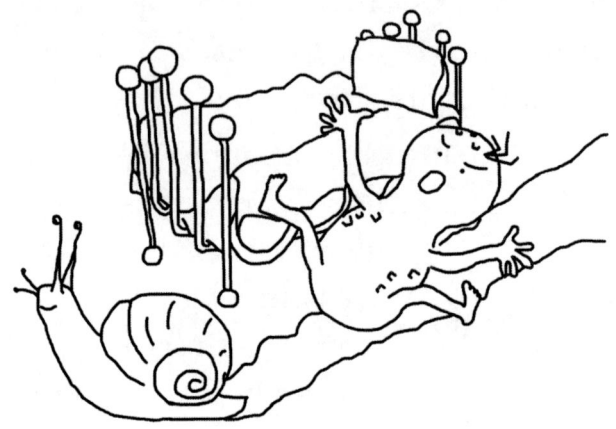

There is another problem, too. When Curly slides around the house, he leaves a slippery trail of slime. As Curly gets bigger, he leaves more slime. The floor is slippery all the time. One morning, the doctor gets out of bed and slips and crashes onto the floor.

"Ow!" he yells. "Curly, stop making this slime!"

Curly looks sad but does not reply. He waves his eyes around, and then his feelers droop. He can't look Dr. Peanut in the face.

That night, the doctor goes on the *Internut* to send a *p-mail* to the giants. He types:

> Dear giants, I don't
> know what to do about
> Curly. He never, ever
> listens!

Curly aims one eye at the screen. Then Curly begins to push the *compeater* keys with his other pair of feelers. He types:

> What does *listen* mean?

"*Listen?*" says the doctor. He picks up his megaphone. "IT MEANS USING YOUR EARS!"

The doctor tugs at his own ear. Curly types:

> What's that?

"THIS THING THAT I'M TUGGING? IT'S MY EAR!" the doctor shouts through his megaphone.

Curly looks puzzled.

Dr. Peanut wonders, "What is going on?"

He decides to give Curly a check-up. He wants to look at Curly's ears. He looks all over Curly's head. Strange! *Pea-culiar!* He can't find any ears on Curly.

"No ears?" the doctor says to himself. He says to Curly, "Curly, can you hear me?"

Curly types:

```
Why do you wiggle your
lips?
```

The doctor laughs. So Curly doesn't listen because he can't hear anyone speak! Then Dr. Peanut feels sad. He types:

```
Curly, how can you be
my peat if we can't
even talk to each
other?
```

Curly waves his eyes and shakes. He seems to be laughing. He types:

> LOL! We are talking
> right now on your
> compeater!

The doctor laughs. "It's true! We are talking by typing. Ha ha!" Then he types:

> But Curly, it is
> peavish when you stay
> up all night making
> noise around the
> house. You make it
> hard for me to sleep.
> And your slime makes
> me fall and hurt
> myself. Can you pease
> turn it off?

Curly replies:

> I can't. I need to
> make the slime. It
> lets me slide around.

He shows the doctor where the slime comes out, from a hole low on his neck.

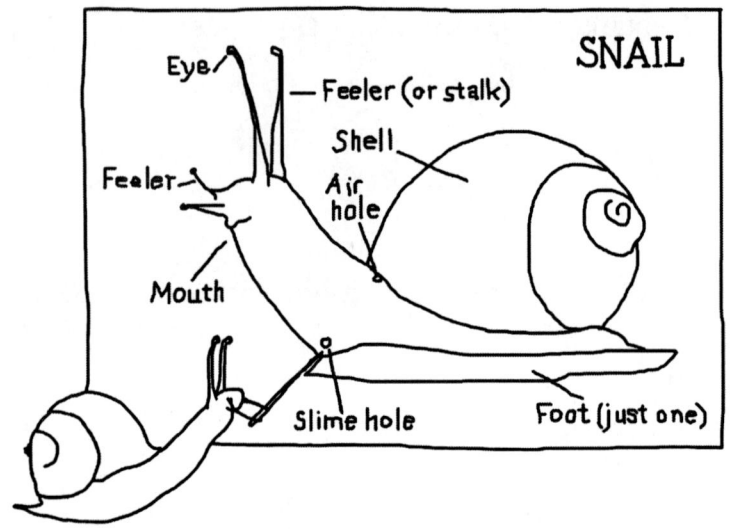

Then Curly types:

> And didn't you know
> that snails stay up
> all night? For us,
> night is better than
> day. At night the air
> is cool and wet, and
> animals that might eat
> us don't see us moving
> around in the dark.
> It's our time to go
> looking for food.

Dr. Peanut replies:

```
I get it. Then I
cannot ask you to
change how you are.
You have taught me
things I needed to
know.
```

Curly types:

```
But I can still be
your friend.
```

The doctor nods and types:

```
That would be nutty,
if you didn't make
that slime.
```

Curly points to the word *nutty*.

```
What does that word
mean?
```

The doctor replies:

```
Nutty means good in
giant talk. Don't you
say "nutty" too?
```

Curly shakes his head. He types:

> Of course not. In
> Slime Language, we
> always write, "Slimy."

Dr. Peanut laughs and types:

> Slimy! What a great
> word for nutty.

Curly nods.

> Yes. But most of the
> time, we don't write
> it down. In Slime
> Language, mostly we
> talk by making signs
> with our feelers. I
> will teach you some
> Slime Language if you
> like.

The doctor types:

> Nutty!

For days, Curly and the doctor try
to fix the problem of the slippery slime.
Whenever Curly slides around the house,

Dr. Peanut tries to wipe the floor behind him, but soon the doctor's knees feel *peavish* from too much crawling around.

Curly tries dragging a towel behind himself, but pretty soon all the towels are soggy. Dr. Peanut has to wash and dry towels all day.

Dr. Peanut tries wearing *pealows* all over himself, so he won't hurt himself when he falls. But he always seems to fall on the place where he wasn't wearing a *pealow,* so he's always yelling, "Ow!"

Curly tries riding a skateboard, but he crashes down the stairs.

So nothing works.

Peavish!

Then Curly thinks up a *nutty* idea. By now, the doctor knows enough *Slime Language* so that they can talk to each other by waving.

Curly waves his feelers to say, "Dr. Peanut, I will live in your yard. Then I won't get slime in the house. Also, if I am outside, I can stay up all night, and you can get your sleep."

Dr. Peanut grins and waves his arms to say, "*Nutty!* You'll be my neighbor instead of my *peat!*"

What does Curly reply to that?

"*Slimy!*"

Chapter 3

Too Many Squirrels

One warm afternoon, Dr. Peanut is doing a check-up. His patient's name is Peaka.

"*Pease* hold still, Peaka," he says. "I need to find out how tall you are."

All at once, the *peanutrician* yawns.

"Sorry!" he says. "I didn't mean to yawn in your face."

"That's okay," says Peaka. "Do you get enough sleep at night?"

"Thanks for asking," he replies. "Yes, I sleep well, ever since Curly moved out of my house. I don't know why I'm feeling sleepy."

"You work too hard," she says. "Why don't you quit work early  today? Go out and have some fun."

"That's a *nutty* idea," says the doctor. "Maybe some fresh air will wake me up."

After Peaka is gone, Dr. Peanut goes out for a run by the park. He takes his *p-phone*, in case someone calls. He also takes his megaphone, in case he needs to tell some giant that he is one of the talking peanuts. The sun is hot, so he wears the megaphone like a hat.

In the park, some giants are kicking a ball. Dr. Peanut wants to go in and cheer, but the park is full of squirrels.

And we *know* what squirrels will eat.

But Dr. Peanut does not act afraid. He thinks, "I will be brave! I won't let my fear keep me out of the park."

The doctor sneaks inside the gate. He gets all the way to a tree, when suddenly a squirrel appears. She stops and stands up to fix her beady eyes on him.

"Uh-oh!" thinks Dr. Peanut.

He tries to run but the squirrel is too fast. She jumps in front of him and tries to grab him with her paws. Dr. Peanut hits her on the nose. She jumps away. But then she comes back. She chases him down and grabs him and sticks him in her cheek.

"Put me down!" the doctor shouts. He tries to sound strong.

But the squirrel does not do as she is told. She has big ears, but she does not seem to understand. Dr. Peanut wishes he could talk to this squirrel, but he can't because he doesn't know any *Squirrelish*, and the squirrel does not know *Pinglish*.

The squirrel runs across the grass with Dr. Peanut in her mouth. Then she stops and scratches at a spot in the ground. She starts to dig a hole.

"What are you doing?" the doctor yells.

"*Squeak!*" she replies. She drops him in the hole and starts to pile dirt on top of him.

"This is strange," the doctor thinks. "This is *pea-culiar*."

It is certainly not what he expected. He expected to be eaten! Then he remembers

some science. He remembers a fact about squirrels. He remembers that sometimes squirrels save their food for later instead of eating it right away. They bury it in the ground.

The doctor decides to let himself be buried.   Then, when the squirrel leaves, he will dig himself out and escape.

Soon the squirrel has finished her work. The doctor hears her walking away. A moment later, he digs himself out.

But the squirrel has not gone far. She sees him pop out of the hole, and she bounces back and grabs him again.

"Stop doing that!" the doctor yells.

She stuffs him back in the hole. She throws the dirt back on top of the doctor and stamps it down with her paws.

"This is *peavish!*" thinks Dr. Peanut. "Every time she sees me get out, she wants to bury me again. I must wait until she's really gone! I might as well take a nap."

But then he remembers a scientific fact about peanuts: a peanut who stays in the ground too long will sprout and turn into a plant!

"I need to dig out soon!" he thinks.

He waits until it seems like forever. Then he digs himself a little way out. He still doesn't see any squirrel, so he digs himself out all the way.

He still doesn't see any squirrel. But then he sees a shadow on the grass. He looks up and sees the squirrel waiting on a branch!

She jumps down and stuffs him back in her cheek. She starts to bury him again.

Then she changes her mind and stops. Instead, she carries him up the tree.

The squirrel's nest is in the tree, and in the nest are three small kits. (In science, a baby squirrel is called a "kit.")

"Look what I brought!" the mother squeaks to her kits in Squirrelish.

The kits don't know what to think. They have never seen a peanut. They think maybe the doctor is a toy. They roll him around and try to grab him from each other.

"Stop!" the doctor orders.

Now the mother looks upset. She grabs the doctor away from the kits. She plans to show them how to crack a peanut with their teeth.

"It's now or never!" thinks Dr. Peanut. He grabs a leaf and sticks it in the mother's nose.

"*Squeash!*" she sneezes.

Her sneeze blows the doctor out of the nest. As the doctor begins to fall, he grabs the biggest leaf he can reach. The leaf slows down his fall, and the doctor lands all right in the grass.

But the squirrel runs down to get him back. He has just enough time to dive under a trash bin. She tries to reach him under the bin, but she can't quite grab him in her paws.

"Go away!" the doctor yells.

Then he remembers his *p-phone*. He takes it out and calls his giant friends.

"Help!" he cries.

"Hi, Dr. Peanut," says the boy. "Where are you?"

"In the park!"

"We're in the park, too," says the boy. "We're looking around, but we don't see you anywhere. Can you wave a flag or something?"

"I can't," says the doctor. "I'm under a

trash bin near the field. I'm being attacked by a squirrel!"

"We'll be right there," says the boy.

The giants run to the bin. They chase the squirrel away and brush the dirt off the doctor.

"Thanks!" he says. "That was close!"

"Those squirrels are awfully big for you," says the girl. "Were you trying to catch one for a *peat*?"

"No," he replies. "Squirrels are much too *peavish* for that!"

The kids take the doctor home on their bike. It is evening when they set him down at his door. Curly the snail is just getting up for the night.

When the giants are gone, Curly waves his feelers to say in *Slime Language*, "Are you okay? You look banged up."

Dr. Peanut smiles. "Maybe a little," he waves. "But don't worry, I'm as *nutty* and *slimy* as always. Still, you won't believe what almost happened!"

Chapter 4

Where Peanuts Come From

When peanut kids need a check-up, they go to see a *peanutrician*. They go to Dr. Peanut who checks their arms and legs and shells. He checks their eyes and noses and throats.

To test their hearing, he tells them jokes. If they laugh, then he knows that they can hear. This is the joke he likes to tell: "Don't stay out in the sun too long, or you may roast!"

Then he watches to see if they laugh. What he said is a joke because peanuts do not really roast in the sun. If a peanut kid doesn't laugh, Dr. Peanut tries asking a riddle like this: "Do you know what giants do if you're a roasted peanut?"

"What?"

"Eat you! Ha ha!"

Some peanut kids laugh at that because they like to be scared. Some kids don't laugh because they don't like to be scared. In that case, the doctor tickles them to make sure they know how to laugh.

Dr. Peanut likes to know about things, and he likes to answer questions. He is very fond of science. That's why the peanut kids hang around his office. They can ask him anything, and he will tell them all he knows. One day, Peaka is there, along with her tall friend, Peasha, and her short friend, Peaber.

Peaka asks him, "Dr. Peanut, where do baby peanuts come from?"

"Good question, Peaka," says the

Peaka   Peasha   Peaber

peanutrician. "Step up close and I will show you some *peactures.* Look at this one. It's a *peacture* of a peanut plant. Can you see its flowers?"

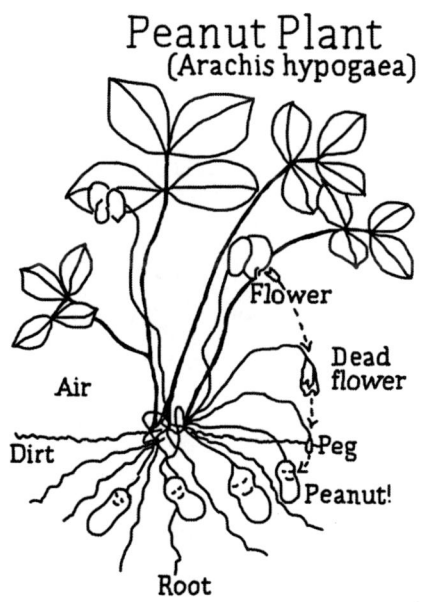

Peanut Plant
(Arachis hypogaea)

Flower

Dead flower

Air

Dirt

Peg

Peanut!

Root

"Yes," the kids reply.

"*Nutty*," he says. "When a peanut flower dies, its stem bends down to the dirt. The tip of the stem dips into the ground. Now the tip is called a peg. When the peg is in the ground, a new peanut grows there, underground."

Peasha laughs. "Doc, are you making this up?" he asks. "Who ever heard of a flower that sticks itself in the ground!"

"No, I am telling you what really happens," the doctor replies. "I am telling you science."

Then Peaber speaks up. He says, "The giant kids know their parents. How come I don't know my parents?"

"Well, that peanut plant is your parent," says the doctor. "And you also do have *pea-rents*, as we say in *Pinglish*."

Peasha raises his hand and asks, "What's the difference between *pea-rents* and parents?"

"That's easy," replies Dr. Peanut. "The

difference is that *pea-rent* has an extra letter *e*! Ha ha!"

"Stop joking," says Peaka. "What's the difference that matters the most?"

"Well," says the doctor, "giant babies are born from their parents, but peanut babies are not born from *pea-rents*. *Pea-rents* are just older peanuts who look after younger ones and love them. Peanut babies are born from a plant, just like the *peacture* shows."

"Then where are the plants?" asks Peaber. "Why don't we see them where we live?"

"That's because they're out on farms where the giants grow peanuts. They grow millions of peanuts out there."

"Then why don't we have millions of peanuts with us?" asks Peaber. "Why are there only a few of us here?"

"That's because the rest get roasted," says the doctor.

"Roasted?!"

"Yes, roasted and eaten."

"*Peavish! Peavish!*" scream the kids.

"Now, now," says Dr. Peanut. "It's not so bad. You see, once a year, we sneak out to the farm when the giants are digging up a crop of peanuts. When the peanuts come out of the ground, we grab a few babies and run! We bring them back to our homes and raise them so that they grow

arms and legs and learn to speak *Pinglish*.
And that's how each of us is born."

"Gosh," says Peasha. "What a *nutty*
way to be born!"

Peaka gives the doctor a look. "Is all
this really true?" she asks.

"Of course!" he replies. "Some day
I'll take you when we go to the farm. It's
exciting to save baby peanuts!"

Dr. Peanut shows them another
peacture. He says,
"Look at this giant. He
is a famous peanut
farmer. His name is
Jimmy Carter."

"Why is he famous?" Peaber asks.

Dr. Peanut smiles and says, "Because
once, a long, long time ago, he was also
the president of the giants. And after he
was done with that, he went out and built
houses for homeless giants."

"Where did you get that *peacture* of
him?" asks Peaka.

"I got it from my giant friends," says Dr. Peanut. "But I don't know why it says '25 cents.' Maybe that's his nickname."

"Wow," says Peasha. "I'd love to meet 25 cents. And I love to learn these things. History is so *nutty*."

"And so is science!" Peasha says. "But is it true that dead peanut flowers stick their heads into the ground?"

"Yes," says Dr. Peanut, "because science is *nutty*. *Nutty* and true."

Chapter 5

The C-in-P Machine

"Is everyone okay today?" Dr. Peanut asks the kids. "Peasha, you look a little *peavish*. Is something wrong?"

Peasha answers, "I'm not sick, but I do have a problem."

"What?"

"I'm too tall."

The doctor nods. "You are tall, Peasha. It must be *peavish* if you don't like being the way you are. But what is wrong with being taller than other peanuts?"

Peasha replies, "One problem is that other kids keep asking me, 'Peasha, Peasha, why are you so tall?' I get tired of saying I don't know why."

Dr. Peanut turns to Peaka and Peaber. He asks them, "What do you think?" Can we help tall Peasha with his problem?"

"I think we can," says Peaka. "We can paint the top of Peasha purple. Then he will look like a shorter peanut who is carrying a grape on his head."

"*Nutty*," says Dr. Peanut. "Peasha, would you like to be painted?"

But he already knows how Peasha
will answer, because all peanuts like to
be painted. Even Dr. Peanut likes to be
painted.

"*Pease!*" says Peasha. "Paint me!"

Dr. Peanut gets out some cans of paint.
They paint the top of Peasha to look like a
grape. They also paint a face on Peasha's
middle, below the grape.

Peasha looks at himself in a mirror.

"I'm not so sure about this," he says. "Maybe this isn't a *nutty* idea. What if the giants like to eat grapes?"

"True," says the doctor.

They wash off the paint. Peasha looks in the mirror for a second time and says, "But now I look too tall again."

"I have another idea," says the doctor. "We will look at you in my new machine. It is called the *C-in-P machine*. I just invented it this week. Everyone *pease* come into my lab."

They all go into the doctor's lab, where he keeps his *C-in-P machine*.

Dr. Peanut says, "Peasha, take off your

shoes and socks and get inside."

Peasha looks worried. "Is it dangerous?"

"No," says the doctor.

Peasha takes off his shoes and socks and gets inside the *C-in-P machine*. The doctor turns it on. The machine hums. Soon, a big screen shows what is inside Peasha.

"So what do we see inside Peasha?" Dr. Peanut asks the other peanut kids.

"We see kernels," says Peaber.

"How many?" asks the doctor.

"Three."

"Yes," the doctor replies. "Peasha has three kernels."

From inside the *C-in-P machine*, Peasha asks, "How many kernels do other peanuts have?"

"Most have two kernels," says the doctor. "That's why you are taller, Peasha. You can come out now."

Peasha gets out.

"Peaber, you go next," says Dr. Peanut.

"Nutty!" says Peaber. He takes off his shoes and socks and climbs into the *C-in-P*.

"Now what do we see?" asks Dr. Peanut.

"We see only one kernel," says Peaka. "Is that why Peaber is short?"

"*Nutty* thinking," the doctor replies.

"Why don't I have more kernels?" Peaber asks from inside the machine. "Is something wrong with me?"

"No," says the doctor. "You are *peafect* like the rest of us. As *peafect* today as the day when they dug you out of the ground. It's just the way you were made."

"But having one kernel is short," says Peaber as he gets out of the *C-in-P*.

"I can think of one *nutty* thing about it," says Peasha. I bet you can go to a movie and pay half price."

"It's true," says Peaber. "I only pay half as much as other peanuts."

"Now," says the doctor, "can anyone guess why my new machine is called the *C-in-P*?"

The peanut kids think a long time.

"Wait, don't tell me!" says Peaka. "I know. I know!"

"Then tell us why," says the doctor.

"Oops, I forget," she says. "Wait! I know! I know. It's because the machine can see inside peanuts. Ha! Ha!"

Dr. Peanut laughs, too, and says,

"Right. Would you like to get in now?"

"No, thanks," she says. "I can guess what it will show me."

"But what about my problem?" says tall Peasha. "I need to find out something *nutty* about being so tall."

"Well," says Peaka, "You can help us reach things that are way high up."

"And you can help us see over fences," says Peaber.

"But here is the best part," says Dr. Peanut. "Some of us are just *nutty*. Others of us are *double-nutty*. But having three kernels makes you *triple-nutty!*"

62

Chapter 6

Ask
Before You Bite

One day, Peasha and Peaka carry Peaber into the doctor's office. Poor Peaber is moaning.

"Ohhhh!" he moans. He looks like he has been bitten.

"Doctor," says Peasha, "a giant picked Peaber up from a nap, and almost ate him!"

"How *peavish!*" says Dr. Peanut. "Peaber, you are lucky to still be alive. How did you escape from being eaten?"

Peaber answers, "I screamed and the giant put me down. But now I feel awful."

"Be careful, doctor," says Peaka. "We think his shell is cracked."

Dr. Peanut gives Peaber a check-up. Peaka is right. Peaber's shell is dented and cracked. Dr. Peanut takes Peaber into his lab and puts Peaber inside the *C-in-P machine* so they can look at Peaber's kernel.

"You are lucky your kernel is still okay," the doctor says. "But I will need to put you in a cast."

He puts a cast on Peaber.

Then he says, "In six weeks, we can take off the cast and your shell will be *nutty* again."

That night, Dr. Peanut sends *p-mails* to many other peanuts. He types:

```
Friends, we need
to hold a meeting.
There's too much
biting going on! Pease
come to my office
tomorrow night.
```

The next night, everyone comes to the meeting, and Peaber tells what happened.

"Friends," says Dr. Peanut, "we need to make sure that the giants don't bite us anymore by mistake. In this meeting, let us think about how to do that."

One peanut *pea-rent* stares at Peaber. She feels very angry because of his bite. In fact, she is *peaved*!

She yells, "Let's pull out all the giants' teeth!"

The rest of the peanuts are silent. They are not sure what to say.

"Let's not get too angry," says Dr. Peanut. "I have some *nutty* giant friends. I'm sure they would not like to lose all their teeth. Wouldn't *you* be unhappy if *you* couldn't eat? We don't want to make things worse."

He looks around the room and asks, "Can anyone think of something else?"

Another peanut starts to cry. He says, "Let's all run away!"

Another peanut lady is *peaved* and wants to get even. She says, "Let's cover ourselves with hot pepper so the giants will burn their mouths when they bite us!"

"Hmm," says the doctor. "Some giants *like* spicy food. Let's hear some more ideas. Let's write them all down on a flip chart, so everyone can read them. Then we can talk about them and vote on what we should do."

"I'll write!" says Peaka.

Another peanut raises a hand and says, "First, we should all carry megaphones."

"Peaka, write that down," says the doctor, so Peaka writes it down.

"Here is my idea," another peanut says. "If you nap in the park, put a sign on yourself that says, 'Giants, do not eat me. I am only asleep.'"

Peaka writes down that one, too.

"*Nutty*," says the doctor. "More ideas?"

One after another, more of the talking

peanuts speak. Each one has a different idea.

One says, "Let's tell the giants we're moldy and rotten. Then none of them will want to eat us."

Another says, "Let's paint ourselves green all over with red and yellow spots. The giants won't eat green peanuts with spots, and painting each other is fun!"

"I have an idea," says Peaber. "Let's make big signs for the giants to read. The signs will tell them not to bite us."

The peanuts talk about all the ideas. Then they vote for making signs. The next day, signs pop up everywhere in the giants' town.

Would you eat a giant?
No?
Then do not eat
a talking peanut!

Look out, giants.
We're getting
peaved!

The peanut kids also make *P-shirts*.
Then Dr. Peanut calls his giant friends.

"Are the giants getting our message?"
he asks.

"What message?" says the girl. "Did
you send us a *p-mail*?"

"I mean our signs," he says.

"What signs?" she asks.

"There must be some problem," he tells
her. "May I come for a visit?"

"Sure."

Dr. Peanut goes to the giants' house. He takes Peaber along.

"See what some careless giant has done to poor Peaber?" the doctor says.

"We're really sorry," says the boy. "Peaber, you look *peavish*."

"I am," says Peaber. "*Peavish* and *peaved*!"

He tells the boy and girl what happened. They cry and give him a flower and make him a *get-nutty card*.

The doctor says, "I don't know why our signs didn't work. How can we make sure that no more talking peanuts get bitten?"

"Well," says the girl, "there are some problems. One is that a lot of giants don't know that there are two kinds of peanuts, and some of them know but forget. And it is hard for them to know what is a talking peanut and what is not the talking kind, unless the peanut yells. And some of our friends just don't believe there is such a thing as a talking peanut. You should come to our class and teach about it, so they can see for themselves."

"We would love to," says the doctor.

The next day, Dr. Peanut and Peaber go to the giants' school. To be safe, the doctor wears a P-shirt. He starts by showing the class how peanut plants grow. He tells them about 25 cents.

"Who's that?" they ask.

"You know," he replies. "I mean Jimmy Carter, the peanut farmer."

He tells them where talking peanuts come from. He tells them everything he told the peanut kids. He says it all with a megaphone, so even the teacher can hear.

A boy raises his hand and asks, "Doctor, do peanuts have belly buttons?"

"What kind of buttons?" the doctor asks.

"Belly buttons," the boy repeats.

"What's a belly button?" asks the doctor. "Is it a button you sew on your belly?"

The students laugh.

The teacher says, "Class, please don't laugh at the doctor."

"That's okay," says Dr. Peanut. "I don't mind."

The boy says, "Every kid has a belly button. It's the place where we used to have a cord, inside our mothers before we were born."

"Oh," says the doctor. "Now I know what you mean. But peanuts are different.

Before I was dug up, I grew at the end of a stem of a plant. It held me right at the top of my head. That's why we don't have belly buttons. We have *peg buttons*, instead."

He shows his *peg button* to the class.

Some kids say, "Ugh!"

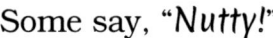

Peg button

Some say, "*Nutty!*"

Some say, "Doctor, *pease* tell us more science."

So Dr. Peanut tells them more. He says, "You giants raise peanuts for food. In other words, you eat us."

Some giant kids lick their lips. Others begin to cry.

One says, "Doctor, I will never eat peanuts again!"

"*Pease* don't say that," the doctor replies. "Eating peanuts is *nutty* for giants. And roasted peanuts do not mind being eaten. They don't feel a thing. And it is part of how peanut plants make their way

73

in the circle of life. But be careful what you eat. *Talking* peanuts don't want to be eaten. Before you eat a peanut, be sure that it is not one of us."

"But how can we be sure?" someone asks.

"First, hold it close to your ear and see if it can talk. Also, look for a face or arms and legs."

A girl raises her hand and asks, "Dr. Peanut, why don't you peanuts put up signs to tell us not to eat you?"

"Your eyes need a check-up," says the doctor. "You must need glasses. We put up signs all over town. Look out the window. We put one right there in the grass."

The giants run to the window to look. Then they laugh. "Dr. Peanut, that sign is too small for us!"

That afternoon the class makes a *get-nutty card* for Peaber. They also write their names on his cast. Then Dr. Peanut,

Peaber and the students paint a banner and hang it outside the school.

After class, Dr. Peanut takes off Peaber's cast, and Peaber's shell is *peafect* again. That night, Dr. Peanut opens his *compeater* to watch peanut *PV*. Then he changes to giant TV to see some giant news. The giant students are on TV. They are waving their banner and singing.

Don't eat the talking peanuts!

Eat roasted peanuts instead!

A giant parent walks by their banner and says, "These kids! They don't even know how to spell the word *please*!"

Dr. Peanut laughs and says, "Oh, yes they do. In *Pinglish*!"

Memoir and fiction
from One Monkey Books

The Room
by John M. Brewer, Jr.

The memoir of a 1960s Pittsburgh high school
rebellion against
a legendary "win-
ning" coach. Some
talented play-
ers joined the
Westinghouse
Bulldogs. Others
wisely avoided this
champion team.
Humorously,
compassionately,
unflinchingly,
Brewer tells how he
submitted for glory,
battled for truth,
and did his part in
closing down the
reign of a damaging coach.

"Fascinating cover to cover."
–*Midwest Book Review*

Ratting on Russo
a novel
by Alan Venable

Poor Marty Badger. Of all the wet-winged critters emerging from rusty, post-war Pittsburgh

soil, whose rever-
ence for Jimmy
Doolittle's Tokyo
raiders and the
1950 bullet-nosed
Studebaker ran
deeper than Mar-
ty's? Yet whose
coming of age had
turned crueler?
Whose bodily parts
more rebellious?
Whose pubescent
classmates more
annoying? Whose
music further out
of step? Whose
sense of wonder
more perplexed? Misdeeds more delinquent?
Love more hopeless? That is, whose not count-
ing Russo's?

A lifelong lover of peanuts, Alan Venable is also the author of more than thirty books for children and young adult readers and several children's plays, as well as novels and plays for adults. He lives in San Francisco.

CPSIA information can be obtained at www.ICGtesting.com
Printed in the USA
BVOW03s1418280114

343110BV00006B/9/P